Watch Out!
Runaway Roller Skates!

Missy and Baby strolled down the street. The neighborhood looked nice enough, although there weren't many big trees around. Her old neighborhood had had better trees.

"Watch out!" someone shouted from behind them. Missy turned to see a girl about her own age on roller skates. "Move your dog!" the girl shouted.

Missy reached down to shove Baby aside, but she wasn't quick enough. The girl crashed into Baby and fell smack on her backside. "Ouch!" she said.

It wasn't *exactly* the first impression that Missy had wanted to make. But she helped the girl up, held out her hand, and said, "Hi! I'm Missy Fremont!"

BEST FRIENDS

by Molly Albright

illustrated by Dee deRosa

Troll Associates

Library of Congress Cataloging in Publication Data

Albright, Molly.
   Best friends.

   Summary: Unhappy with her family's move to a new
city and after a disastrous first week at her new
school, twelve-year-old Missy is convinced that her best
and only friend is her dog Baby.
   [1. Moving, Household—Fiction.   2. Schools—Fiction.
3. Friendship—Fiction.   4. Dogs—Fiction.
5. Adoption—Fiction]   I. deRosa, Dee, ill.   II. Title.
PZ7.A325Be   1988   [Fic]   87-13874
ISBN 0-8167-1151-8 (lib. bdg.)
ISBN 0-8167-1152-6 (pbk.)

A TROLL BOOK, published by Troll Associates,
Mahwah, NJ 07430

Printed in the United States of America.

10 9 8 7 6 5 4 3 2 1

BEST FRIENDS

CHAPTER

1

"**A**ha!" cried Melissa Fremont. "Found them!" She pulled two photo albums out of a cardboard box packed high with books. Then she eased herself down on her bedroom floor next to Baby, her Old English sheepdog. "Now for one last look at our life in Cincinnati," she said solemnly.

It was Saturday, and moving day in the Fremont household. Missy was all packed. Her room was empty except for a few boxes and bags on which she had written PROPERTY OF MELISSA FREMONT. Her rug had been rolled up and was ready for the movers.

Missy sat cross-legged on the floor and slowly leafed through her album. It was a glossy brown book with MY FAMILY printed in gold-colored lettering on the cover. Baby barked and wagged his stubby tail. Missy looked at him and grinned. "Okay, okay, I get the message," she told him. "We'll look at *your* book in a minute."

She turned back to her album and studied a faded photograph of a smiling man and woman holding a tiny baby. Underneath, she had written, "Mom, Dad, and Me."

"This is when Mom and Dad first picked me up at the adoption agency," she told Baby. "I was only five weeks old, and you weren't even born."

Baby barked appreciatively and licked Missy's hand. He'd heard the story many times before of how he and Missy were both special because they had been *chosen*. Missy sometimes wondered about the people who had given her up. But not often. She was very happy with her parents—and with Baby. Baby was Missy's best friend. They even looked alike. Missy had shaggy, curly red hair that fell into her eyes just like Baby's gray fur.

Missy turned to the back of the album and laughed. "Remember this?" she said. It was a picture of Missy with her arm in a cast. "I'll bet I'm the only person ever to break an arm by just falling off a bed." Melissa was not too coordinated. "Klutzy" was the word.

Missy picked up Baby's photo album next. "Here's *your* adoption picture," she said, pointing. "You were eight weeks old when I chose you, and I was seven years old. You were so tiny, I named you Baby."

Missy leaned over and kissed the top of Baby's head. The dog stretched his enormous paws and yawned. "*Now* look at you," said Missy with a laugh. "You're a giant."

She closed the album, looked around her empty bedroom, and sighed. "I wish we didn't have to move, don't you?" she said. "What if we don't like Indianapolis?"

Baby whined and lay down on the floor with his head between his paws. Cincinnati was the only home either of them had ever known. Now Missy's father, a viola player, had taken a new job in a new city.

"I know being first viola with the Indianapolis Symphony is better than being second viola with the Cincinnati Symphony," she said. "But I still don't think it's fair. What about us? I'm going to miss Kelly and Susan, and I have to leave Irving Elementary and Grandma. And you won't have Winnie-the-Poodle to play with anymore. It's just not fair," she said again.

Mrs. Fremont poked her head inside the door. She was carrying a stack of bath towels. "What's not fair?" she asked.

"That we have to leave," Missy replied. "Baby and I like it here. Besides, the house looks weird without furniture."

"We'll have all our furniture back tonight," Missy's mother said with a smile. "And just wait until you see your new bedroom. You'll love it!"

Missy shook her head. "I don't know about that."

"I want you to make a final check in here," Mrs. Fremont continued. "Your father's almost finished packing the car, and we want to leave in an hour."

Missy got up off the floor. She carefully placed the photo albums back into the cardboard box and closed the flap. She had so many memories of her room!

"Remember when I didn't want to take swimming lessons and we hid underneath the bed?"

Missy said to Baby. "Mom would never have found me if you hadn't sneezed."

Baby barked and shook his back end.

"And how about the time we spilled the pitcher of grape juice?" Missy looked over at the large purple blotch near the doorway. "I made you sit on the blotch so Mom wouldn't notice, and then you had purple fur for a month!"

Missy looked sadly around the room. "I wonder who's going to be living in this room next? Maybe it'll be another kid with a dog."

From downstairs, Missy heard her father honking the car horn. She ran over and leaned out the window. "Coming," she yelled. She took one last look around the room. "Good-by, room," she said. "It's been great."

Mr. Fremont was already starting to back out of the driveway. "Stop, Dad," yelled Missy as she and Baby ran toward the car. "You're forgetting your wife and daughter!" Baby gave several loud barks. "And Baby!" Missy added breathlessly.

Mr. Fremont grinned and threw on the brakes. "I thought it seemed awfully quiet in here," he said. "Hop aboard, you two. Your mother's still inside."

Missy and Baby climbed into the back seat, where Missy had already arranged everything she would need for the trip. She and Baby had two pillows each, and a bag of snacks: raisins and carrot sticks for Missy; hard-boiled eggs for Baby—his all-time favorite. Baby also had a rawhide bone to chew on, and Missy had brought along a new paperback mystery to read.

"Looks like you're settled in for a trip to California," Mr. Fremont said. "We're going only about a hundred miles, you know."

Missy smiled and rolled her eyes. Sometimes her father could be so silly. "Of course I know how far we're going," Missy told him. "I just like to be prepared." She leaned over the front seat. "And speaking of being prepared," she added quickly, "where are your glasses, Dad?" Her father had a habit of misplacing things.

Mr. Fremont touched his temples. "Oh, no," he groaned. "What did I do with those darn things?"

He jumped out of the car and started to look around. The next thing Missy knew, he was tapping her window and waving his glasses. "Left them on top of the car," he said with a grin.

As Mr. Fremont settled himself behind the wheel again, Missy's mother approached the car. She looked as if she'd been crying. "Oh, William," she said. Mr. Fremont held her hand and for a moment nobody said anything. They all just sat quietly and looked at the house.

"Well," Mr. Fremont said finally, "I guess we'd better be on our way."

"Good-by and good luck!" called their next-door neighbors.

"Have a safe trip!" shouted their neighbors from across the street.

"Good-by!" replied the Fremonts.

Missy opened her window, and she and Baby hung out as far as they could. "Good-by, Cincinnati," Missy called. "Hello, Indianapolis."

E ven with a stop for hot fudge sundaes, the drive to Indianapolis took only two and a half hours. Mr. Fremont was on the fourth verse of "Michael, Row the Boat Ashore," when Missy interrupted him.

"Dad," she said, "tell me what the house looks like again. I want to try to pick it out."

"Well," he replied, "it's a two-story house, yellow brick on the outside, and it's surrounded by lots of nice shrubs."

Missy thought it sounded pretty ugly, but she didn't want to hurt her father's feelings.

"What about the inside?" she said. She wanted to picture everything.

"It's got a big living room with a real fireplace, a kitchen, a dining room, three bedrooms, and three baths," said Missy's mother.

"And I get my own bathroom, right?" Missy asked.

"Right," said Mrs. Fremont. "So you can stay in the tub as long as you like." Lately, Missy had gotten into the habit of tying up the bathroom by taking long bubble baths.

"Will Baby like the yard?" Missy asked. When Baby heard his name, he perked up his ears and looked at Missy.

"Absolutely," said Mr. Fremont. "And there's a park at the end of the street where you two can go for long walks."

Mr. Fremont put on his turn signal. "This is our exit," he said. Baby sat up attentively. "You can start looking for the house now."

Missy stared at the neighborhood. "It's so flat here," she said. "Cincinnati had nice hills." She tried to look for kids her own age, but saw only a few small children playing in a yard.

"Do you see the house yet?" Mr. Fremont asked. He turned down a small side street.

"Sixty-fifth Street?" said Missy, reading the sign. "What kind of a street name is that?" She saw several two-story houses. One was painted white and had beautiful ivy crawling all over the front. Then she looked to her right. "That's it!" she said, pointing to a yellow house. "The little one, right?"

"Right," said Mr. Fremont. "That's our house."

Baby stood up and barked loudly. "Down, Baby," Missy said. "We're almost there."

Mr. Fremont pulled slowly into the driveway. "Home sweet home," he said. "Everybody out."

"Look!" said Mrs. Fremont excitedly. "The movers are already here."

Missy watched as three men carried the living-room sofa past her car door.

Mrs. Fremont stuck her head out the car window. "Please be careful with that sofa," she pleaded. "It's an antique."

A man smoking a big cigar looked at her and nodded. "Don't worry, lady," he wheezed. "We'll take good care of it."

Missy opened the back door, and she and Baby tumbled out. Baby immediately headed for the shrubs. "We'll be inside, Mom," Missy called. "Come on, Baby. Let's explore our new house."

Missy decided to check out the kitchen first. It was large and sunny, with a big window overlooking the back yard. The counters were already covered with packing cases marked FRAGILE—DISHES. Missy checked to see if there was anything in the refrigerator. There wasn't.

"Let's go find our room, Baby," she said. They walked through the dining and living rooms and up the stairs. Missy already knew which room was hers and which was the guest room. Her room was the one next to the bathroom—her bathroom.

Missy stepped into her new bedroom and stopped short, staring. "Oh, no!" she gasped. "There must be a mistake!"

Mrs. Fremont ran into the room. "What are you talking about?" she said.

Missy pointed to the walls. "This can't be my room," she said. "Look at the wallpaper!"

Mrs. Fremont studied the walls. They were covered with little blue ducks and green teddy bears carrying umbrellas. "I think it's sort of cute," Mrs. Fremont replied.

"Cute?" Missy wailed. "How can you say that? This bedroom must have belonged to a *baby*! I can't invite anyone over to my room if it looks like this."

Baby looked up at Missy and whined.

"See?" said Missy. "Even Baby knows this room is a total disaster."

"Honey," said Mrs. Fremont, "nothing is permanent. We can paint or re-wallpaper your room if you don't like it."

"How about this afternoon?" Missy suggested hopefully.

Mrs. Fremont thought for a minute. "I have a good idea," she said finally. "Why don't you finish looking around the house and then you can take Baby out to explore the neighborhood. We can talk more about this during dinner. Your dad says there's a great pizza place nearby."

"Okay," sighed Missy. It was clear that any further discussion about her room would have to wait.

Missy and Baby stood in the front yard for several minutes. "Which way?" Missy said. Baby looked up at her and then trotted off to the right. Sixty-fifth Street seemed to be a dead end.

Missy could see a gate at the end of the street. The gate opened onto a wide lawn cut halfway by a narrow paved sidewalk. Maybe that was the park her father had talked about. Missy and Baby strolled up the street. The neighborhood looked nice enough, although there weren't many big trees around. Her old neighborhood had had better trees.

"Watch out!" someone shouted behind them.

Missy turned to see a girl about her own age on roller skates. "Move your dog," the girl ordered.

Missy reached down and tried to shove Baby aside, but she wasn't quick enough. The girl crashed into Baby and fell smack on her backside. "Ouch!" she said.

Baby yelped and jumped away.

Missy offered the girl a hand. "I'm sorry," she said. "Sheepdogs aren't very graceful."

The girl didn't smile, and she didn't take Missy's hand. Instead, she just stood up and brushed herself off. "Ruined," she said in a disgusted voice, examining a tiny rip in the seat of her pants.

"I'm really sorry," Melissa repeated. "It doesn't look so bad, though. I bet you can fix it."

Missy noticed that the girl had beautiful, long blond hair and pierced ears with little gold studs. Missy wasn't allowed to have her ears pierced until she was older.

"Oh, well, I guess I'll give them to my little sister," the girl said. "I can't *stand* wearing torn-up clothes."

There was a moment of awkward silence. "I'm Missy Fremont," Missy finally said. "This is my dog, Baby. We just moved here, into the yellow brick house."

"I'm Stephanie Cook." The other girl pulled a comb out of her back pocket and started to comb her hair. "I live in that big house over there." She pointed to the white house with the ivy.

"That figures," thought Missy.

"How old are you?" Stephanie asked.

"Twelve," said Missy.

"Me, too," replied Stephanie. "Do you like to roller-skate?"

"Well, actually, I don't know how," Missy admitted.

"Boy, you really should learn," Stephanie said. "*Everyone* around here goes skating." She raised her arms in an arch above her head like a ballerina, and spun around several times on the tips of her skates.

Missy could feel her cheeks burning. She felt klutzier by the minute. "I'm not too good at sports," she stammered.

"Too bad! My friends and I just *love* sports. Are you going to the Hills Point School?" Stephanie continued.

Missy nodded.

Stephanie looked her up and down. "Well, I hope *another* new girl shows up this year," she said with a sniff. "For *your* sake, that is."

"Why?" Missy asked.

"So that you'll have someone to be best friends with," Stephanie said. "Everyone at Hills Point has a best friend already. The new girls have to pair up among themselves."

"What if I don't want a best friend?" Missy said. She reached down and scratched Baby behind the ears.

"That's fine with me," Stephanie replied with a shrug. "You just won't have anyone to do things with." She stuck her comb into her pocket and skated back up the street. "See you Monday morning at the bus stop," she said, looking over her shoulder. "And don't be late! The bus driver, Mr. Covey, doesn't wait for anyone."

Missy and Baby watched Stephanie until she was out of sight. "Yuck," Missy said. "I hope all the girls at Hills Point aren't that stuck-up." Baby pushed his wet nose against Missy's hand and wagged his tail. Missy bent down and gave him a big kiss. "Don't worry, Baby," she said. "You'll always be *my* best friend. I guess you and I are just two of a kind."

CHAPTER

3

It was late afternoon on Sunday. Missy poked her head down through the door to the basement. "Hey, Dad," she called. "What're you doing?"

Mr. Fremont pushed his glasses back onto his nose and smiled. His viola was tucked under his chin, and he was tuning it up. "I thought I'd try to get in a little practicing before dinner," he replied. "It's nice and quiet down here."

Missy and Baby clattered down the stairs. Mr. Fremont was sitting on a packing crate with his music stand in front of him. A small lamp balanced uneasily on top of the washing machine.

"Have you seen the box with the dog dish in it?" Missy asked. "Baby's getting tired of eating off paper plates."

"I don't blame him," sighed Mr. Fremont. He looked at Missy and smiled. "Excited about school starting tomorrow?" he asked.

"I guess so," Missy replied.

"Have you met any kids in the neighborhood yet?" said her father.

"Just one," said Missy. "Her name is Stephanie." The thought of seeing that horrible showoff on her stupid skates again made Missy shudder. She'd even avoided going out in the front yard all day.

Missy started to move a pile of boxes. "I know that dish is here somewhere," she said.

"Watch out for the lamp!" Mr. Fremont warned. But it was too late. Missy stumbled over the lamp cord and landed on the floor with a thud.

Mr. Fremont jumped out of his chair. "Are you okay?" he said.

Missy got up and rubbed her forehead. "I think so. I banged my head on the edge of the ironing board, though."

Baby whimpered and licked Missy's face.

Mr. Fremont grinned. "Looks like you're going to have a nice bruise there," he said. He gave Missy a hug and kissed her forehead gently. "You sure you're all right?"

Missy smiled and nodded. "Sure, Dad," she replied. "Just being klutzy again."

After dinner, Missy stood in front of her bathroom mirror and frowned. The lump on her forehead had grown.

"Missy," called Mrs. Fremont. "What are you doing? You've been in the bathroom for over an hour."

Missy sat on the edge of the tub and sighed loudly. No matter how she tried combing her hair, it didn't cover the ugly purple bruise.

"Mom," she wailed, "I can't go to my first day of school looking like this. Everyone will think there's something the matter with me."

Mrs. Fremont opened the door. "Let's see," she said.

Missy made a face and looked at her mother.

"It's not so bad," said Mrs. Fremont. "Does it hurt?"

Missy shook her head.

"If you wore a smile on your face, it would look a lot better," said Mrs. Fremont.

"Mother," Missy said with a groan, "please don't talk to me like one of your kindergartners, okay?" Mrs. Fremont was a kindergarten teacher.

"I'm sorry," she said. "You're right."

Missy looked into the mirror again and frowned. Her mother put an arm around Missy's shoulder. "Maybe we can try putting some of my make-up on it."

Missy's face brightened. "That's a great idea! Thanks, Mom!"

"Remind me in the morning," said Mrs. Fremont. She stood up. "Now, why don't you come down and watch some TV before bed? Dad and I were beginning to wonder if you'd drowned in the bathtub!"

The next morning, Missy glanced nervously out the window as she pulled on her sweater. She could already see two or three kids waiting at the bus stop. She ran into the bathroom and combed her hair one last time. With the make-up on and her bangs combed the right way, she could hardly see the bruise.

Mrs. Fremont knocked on the door.

"Come in," said Missy.

"Isn't it time for you to go?" asked her mother.

Missy thought it was funny to see her mother still in her bathrobe. In Cincinnati, Mrs. Fremont had always been dressed for work at the same time Missy was dressed for school. Mrs. Fremont taught kindergarten at Missy's old school. But, because there weren't any openings for teachers in Indianapolis, Mrs. Fremont had to substitute-teach and give piano lessons on Saturdays and after school.

"Do I look okay?" Missy asked.

"Wonderful," said her mother.

Missy ran into the kitchen, where her father and Baby were having breakfast. "'Bye, Dad," she called.

Mr. Fremont looked up from his newspaper. "Whoa, let's have a look at you," he said.

"Oh, Dad," Melissa said with a grimace. She knelt down and gave Baby a big hug. "You be good today," she whispered.

Baby stood up and followed Missy to the door. "No, Baby," she said. "You can't come to school with me. Stay here and keep Mom company."

Baby sat down and wagged his tail.

"Have a good day," Mr. and Mrs. Fremont called out together as Missy raced out the front door and ran across the street. Missy spotted two boys about her age jumping in and out of the bushes. Several younger children were discussing a TV program they'd seen the night before. And there was Stephanie, combing her hair again.

"Hi, Stephanie," Missy said reluctantly.

"Oh, hi." Stephanie hesitated. "Missy, right?"

"Right."

"Well, guess what, Missy, you're in luck," said Stephanie.

"Why?" Missy said.

"Because there's going to be another new girl in school. Her name is Ashley Woods, and she lives near my best friend Emily."

Missy started to interrupt. "But I—"

Stephanie motioned to the cluster of kids waiting for the bus. "Hey, everyone. This is Missy," she announced. "She's *new*."

Missy smiled weakly. She was relieved to see the bus pull up.

"Come with me, Missy," ordered Stephanie, as she marched down the aisle of the bus. "I'll show you where the *older* kids sit." She led Missy to the rear of the bus, which was empty except for a pretty, slightly plump girl with long, dark hair pulled back in a ponytail. "Hi, Emily," Stephanie called to her. Stephanie pointed to an empty seat. "Okay, Missy, you can sit there," she said.

Missy sat down reluctantly. She watched Stephanie plop down next to Emily in the seat ahead of her.

Emily turned around and smiled. "Welcome to Indianapolis, Missy," she said. "Sorry you have to sit by yourself today—"

"But *Ashley* won't be riding the bus until tomorrow," Stephanie interrupted smoothly. "Her mother's driving her to school today."

Missy leaned back in her seat, wishing she didn't have to listen to Stephanie. Then she heard a noise coming from behind her. It wasn't exactly crying, more like whimpering—the way Baby sounded when he was hurt. Missy peeked over her shoulder. The seat behind her was empty.

Then she heard the whimpering again. "Something's back there," she told herself. This time she got up on her knees and leaned over the back of her seat to look.

"BLAAAAAAAAGH!" With a terrible roar, a monster face leaped up at her.

Missy shrieked and jumped back. Her book bag flew out of her hands, into the seat in front of her—just as Stephanie turned around to see what the noise was about. She got the bag right in the face.

Missy grabbed her book bag in midair, trying to snatch it back. Stephanie's head jerked. "OW!" she yelled. "My hair!"

"This can't be happening," Missy thought as she stared.

Stephanie's long blond hair was caught—stuck in the zipper on the side of the bag. "Hold still," Missy told her. "I'll get you loose." She tugged at the zipper.

"What are you—OUCH!" Stephanie said. "You're pulling my hair out!"

Missy gritted her teeth and kept tugging.

"Quit it!" Stephanie yelled. "You're—" Her head suddenly pulled free.

"There," Missy said. "Now you're loose."

Stephanie held her hand to the side of her head. Then she gave another yell and pointed at the bag. "Look what you did!"

Stephanie was free, all right—but a big clump of her hair was still stuck to the zipper on Missy's

bag. "Where's a mirror?" Stephanie demanded. "She's probably made me bald on one side!"

Meanwhile, the monster was laughing like an idiot, pulling at its ears. Its face began moving. It was a rubber mask! When the mask was off, Missy recognized one of the boys who'd been jumping in the bushes. "Ha-ha-ha! That was the best ever!"

Then he stopped laughing and stared at Missy. He brushed her bangs to one side. "Hey, what's that?" he asked.

Stephanie stopped rubbing her head, and turned around to peer at Missy's face. "Ugh! What happened to your forehead?" she gasped.

"Nothing," Missy muttered. She began to wish she were back in Cincinnati.

"Are you wearing *make-up*?" said Stephanie in a shocked voice. Several students turned around in their seats. "Make-up isn't allowed at Hills Point," she said.

Missy slouched farther into her chair. "This is a special situation," she said.

"Hey! Look at Cyclops," said the boy behind her. "She looks even worse than my mask!"

"Cut it out, Adam," Emily said suddenly. "It's not nice to make fun of people."

Missy clenched her jaw and stared out the window. Maybe if she just ignored everyone, they'd stop bothering her. It had been nice of Emily to stick up for her, though.

The bus stopped for the third time since Missy had gotten on.

The back was starting to fill up, but the seat next to Missy remained empty. She felt as though a huge arrow were pointing at her, saying, "Beware of New Girl." She wished she were back home with Baby, or anywhere but on that school bus. Missy was glad when the bus finally pulled up to the front of Hills Point School. When she stood up, Stephanie tugged on her arm. "Follow me," she ordered.

CHAPTER

4

Missy felt herself being swept out of the bus, into the school, and along a corridor. The next thing she knew, she was standing in a brightly decorated classroom. Missy couldn't help but notice that the teacher looked a lot like her mother.

"You're Mrs. Kaufman, aren't you?" said Stephanie sweetly.

"Why, yes," the teacher replied with a smile.

"Good. I was hoping I'd be in your class this year. I'm Stephanie Cook and this is Emily Green. And *this* is Missy Fremont."

"Well, I'm very happy to meet you," the teacher said pleasantly. "Please take a seat at one of the desks."

Stephanie started to arrange the seating order for the entire class. "Emily and I will sit by the window; Christine and Meredith will sit over there . . ."

Missy stalked over to the window and sat down.

"Wait! That's my seat!" Stephanie said.

"I don't see your name written on it," Missy replied. She couldn't believe how bossy Stephanie was!

Stephanie gave her a strange look and then flashed her sweet, phony smile again. "All right," she said. "You and Ashley may take the window seats. Emily and I will sit by the door. That's a better spot anyway."

Missy folded her arms across her chest. The nerve of that Stephanie Cook, giving her *permission* to sit somewhere! No one was going to tell *Missy Fremont* what to do. Especially not *Stephanie Cook*.

By the time the bell rang, every seat in the room had been taken except for one. Mrs. Kaufman was already giving her introductory speech when a weird-looking girl showed up at the door. Her mother was with her.

"That must be Ashley Woods," thought Missy.

Ashley had dark curly hair and small beady eyes. She looked as if she'd been crying.

"Oh, great," thought Missy. "Ashley looks like a total nerd."

"Hello," chirped Ashley's mother. "I'm Beverly Woods. Are you Mrs. Kaufman?"

"Yes, I am."

"I'm *terribly* sorry we're so late," said Mrs. Woods. "Ashley was having an allergy attack. I wanted her to stay home, but she *insisted* on coming to school. You know how these *star* pupils are!"

Ashley gave a pathetic little sniffle and blew her nose.

"Well, I'm glad you could make it, Ashley," said

Mrs. Kaufman. She smiled brightly. "I'm just starting class. Why don't you take that empty seat by the window?"

Ashley slithered behind the back row of desks and slid into the seat next to Missy.

"I really don't want Ashley going outside for recess today," purred Mrs. Woods. "She's such a delicate child, you see."

"Fine," said Mrs. Kaufman. "Thank you for stopping by." She turned back to the blackboard.

Mrs. Woods hovered around the door for a few more seconds, smiling uncertainly. Then she gave Ashley a little wave and disappeared out the door.

"Now, where were we?" asked Mrs. Kaufman.

"Study buddies," replied Stephanie.

"Thank you," said Mrs. Kaufman. "I want each of you to choose a study buddy who will work with you on joint projects throughout the term."

The class began to stir.

"Please discuss it among yourselves at recess and let me know after lunch," said Mrs. Kaufman.

Missy snuck a sidelong glance at Ashley. She was biting her nails and sucking on a throat lozenge.

Ashley raised her hand. "May I change seats?" she asked in a whiny voice. "I'm catching a chill by the window."

Missy rolled her eyes. It was the beginning of September and as hot as July.

Mrs. Kaufman stopped what she was doing. "Of course," she replied. "Why don't you switch with Stephanie Cook? It should be warmer on that side of the room."

Stephanie stood up indignantly. "I don't want to switch!" she said.

"Please do as I ask," replied Mrs. Kaufman firmly.

Stephanie's face went red. She picked up her books with a disgusted snort and stomped across the room.

Missy grinned from ear to ear. "This is a first," she thought. "The first time Stephanie Cook hasn't gotten *exactly* what she wants!"

When the lunch bell rang, all of the girls immediately left the room together to join the cafeteria line.

Missy was left alone with Ashley.

After lunch, Mrs. Kaufman asked the class to divide into pairs and begin the first project. The students were to read a short chapter in their history books about the Pilgrims' landing at Plymouth Rock. Then they were to pretend they were newspaper reporters covering the landing. Each pair of students was to write two reports: one from the Pilgrims' point of view and the other from the Indians' point of view.

History was one of Missy's favorite subjects. She eagerly pulled her chair over to Ashley's desk. "Why don't we divide the job in half?" she suggested. "That should make it go faster. I'll take the Pilgrims' side, okay?"

"Okay," said Ashley, sounding bored. While Missy read, she could see Ashley doodling all over the illustration of the *Mayflower* in her textbook. She added a mustache and glasses to one of the Pilgrim Fathers. Then she drew a bird sitting on the head of one of the Indians peering from the bushes.

"Ashley, aren't you reading?" Missy said finally.

"Reading strains my eyes," Ashley answered.

"Well, why don't you try writing?" Missy suggested.

Ashley sniffed and looked in her desk. "Do you have any paper?"

"With all those tissues in there, I suppose she doesn't have room for school supplies," Missy thought. She handed Ashley a sheet of paper.

"How are we doing, class?" Mrs. Kaufman asked. "You've got about ten more minutes."

Ashley jumped, and her pencil fell to the floor. "The point's broken," she said. "I can't do this."

Missy sighed and gave her pen to Ashley.

But after a few seconds, Ashley stopped writing. She pulled a tissue from her desk and blew her nose. "This is too hard."

"No, it's not. It's easy," Missy said, taking Ashley's paper. Then she saw what Ashley had written.

"I am an Indean. I was in the bushes. A big boat came. People got off. They weren't Indiens. They had funny hats and buckels on there shoes . . ."

"This is *all*?" Missy gasped. "I don't believe this. You spelled 'buckles' and 'their' wrong. Then you spelled 'Indians' two different ways—and neither of them is right."

Ashley shrugged and blew her nose again— louder. Missy bent over, her pencil flying over the paper. She changed Ashley's story to an interview with Chief Watarumpus, about greeting the Pilgrims.

"Mrs. Kaufman," called Stephanie in a voice loud enough for everyone to hear, "Emily and I are finished."

Missy looked up from her paper and started to write even faster, finishing the Indians' side of the story. Finally, she tossed the finished reports onto Ashley's desk. "This is the last time I'm doing this," she said angrily.

"Boy," she thought. "If I let her, Ashley will even borrow my brain."

Missy looked at the clock. Would this day never end?

Ashley sniffed again.

At three-thirty Missy stomped through the front door of her house and threw down her books. Baby rushed to her and put his paws on her shoulders.

"Baby, you're so lucky you don't have to go to school," Missy said. She buried her head in his fluffy coat.

"How'd it go today?" asked her mother.

"Horrible," replied Missy. "A total disaster." She tumbled to the floor, and Baby plopped down on her lap.

"I'm sure it wasn't *that* bad," said Mrs. Fremont.

"Mom! How can you say that? You weren't there!" she exclaimed.

"Well, it takes time to get adjusted to a new school. Did you make any new friends?"

"I'm never going back," said Missy, ignoring her mother's question. "I hate it."

"It's been only one day. Why don't you give it a little more time?"

Missy shook her head. "Why can't we have school right here? You're a teacher. You can teach Baby and me."

Mrs. Fremont smiled sympathetically. "I'm sorry, honey," she said, "but that isn't practical or possible."

Missy pushed Baby off her lap and stood up angrily. "Why is everybody always against me?" she said. She ran to her room and slammed the door.

Missy lay on her bed, crying quietly. She missed her friends and her house and her grandmother. The more she thought about Cincinnati, the more she hated Indianapolis.

There was a faint scratching at the door. "Go away, Baby," said Missy.

Baby whimpered and scratched louder. Missy wiped the tears from her face and opened the door. "What do you want?"

Baby looked up at her and wagged his tail. In his mouth was Missy's photo album.

Missy knelt down and took the album. "Oh, Baby, I'm sorry," she said softly. "It's not your fault I hate school. You're just trying to cheer me up, aren't you?"

Baby licked Missy's face and sat down patiently. Missy opened the book to the first page. "Here I am being picked up at the adoption agency," she began. Baby wagged his tail and barked. "I was five weeks old, and you weren't even born. . . ."

CHAPTER

5

Melissa turned off her alarm clock and buried her face farther into the pillow. She wasn't about to go back to school a second time. She watched the big hand move slowly forward, and tried to fall asleep again.

"Missy!" exclaimed her mother, poking her head into the room. "Why aren't you up yet?"

Missy pulled the covers tighter. "I think I have a stomachache," she replied.

Mrs. Fremont frowned. "You think?"

Missy nodded and gave a convincing little moan. "Maybe I should stay home from school."

"Your father made French toast for breakfast," said Mrs. Fremont.

Missy lowered the covers. "He did?" she said. French toast was her favorite.

"But if you have a stomachache, you shouldn't eat breakfast."

"I feel well enough for French toast," said Missy.

"Then you feel well enough for school," said Mrs. Fremont with a smile. "Hurry up and get dressed."

"But, Mom," Missy protested, "that's not fair." Missy fell back onto her bed.

Baby ran into the room and stuck his furry face under the blankets.

"Go away," said Missy crossly.

But Baby just wagged his tail, pulled the covers back, and tugged on Missy's nightgown. He loved French toast almost as much as Missy did.

"Okay, okay," said Missy with a sigh. "You win. Let's have French toast." She pulled on her clothes and hurried into the kitchen.

Mr. Fremont was singing "Oh, Susannah" and watching the griddle.

"What's the occasion, Dad?" asked Missy. "We never have French toast during the week."

Mr. Fremont piled three pieces onto a plate and handed it to Missy. "Your mom and I thought you could use some cheering up," he said. He tossed a fourth slice into the air and watched Baby catch it and swallow it whole. "Bull's-eye!" he cried.

"William!" said Mrs. Fremont.

"Sorry, honey," he replied. "It slipped off the spatula." He looked at Missy and winked. "You all set for school today?"

"Yes," Missy replied gloomily.

"That's what I like to hear," Mr. Fremont said, as he stacked two more slices of French toast on her plate.

"That's enough," Missy protested.

"Eat up," said her father. "Nothing like French toast to start the day off right."

*　　*　　*

Missy waited in the kitchen until she saw the school bus pull up across the street.

"Hurry up," called Stephanie as Missy ran out the front door.

Missy bolted up the steps of the bus just as the driver was about to close the door. She took a seat in the front.

"Missy, sit back here with us," Emily called.

Missy pretended not to hear. When the bus pulled into school, she got off quickly and hurried to the classroom. She was in her seat and reading when the rest of the class arrived.

"Good morning, students," said Mrs. Kaufman. "Today you're going to start your independent projects."

Missy glanced at Ashley, who was reading a comic book that was tucked inside her math textbook. Missy breathed a sigh of relief. At least she wouldn't get stuck with Ashley Woods again today.

Missy worked quietly at her desk all morning. When the bell rang for lunch, everyone lined up quickly. Missy took her place at the back of the line behind Ashley. She noticed that Ashley was wearing a heavy gauze bandage on her right hand.

"What did you do to your finger?" asked Missy.

"I bent it backward trying to open a jar," Ashley replied. She held her wrist up limply for Missy to see.

The class filed into the cafeteria.

"Do you think you could carry my food on your tray?" Ashley asked. "My hand hurts too much."

"I guess so," Missy answered.

The day's menu was spaghetti and meatballs. Missy carefully placed two plates on her tray. "Do you want the creamed spinach?" she asked politely.

Ashley nodded enthusiastically.

Missy wrinkled her nose and put the spinach on her tray. After she'd added two cartons of milk and two plates of bread and butter, the tray was pretty crowded. But Missy managed to find space for two ice-cream bars.

"No ice cream for me," said Ashley. "It irritates my throat."

Missy shook her head and put one ice cream back.

"I'll meet you at the table," said Ashley.

The girls in Missy's class always sat at the same table. Missy picked up the tray and slowly followed Ashley across the room toward the table. The tray was starting to feel heavy.

Missy headed for an empty spot next to Stephanie. "Be careful," said Stephanie sharply. "You're about to spill your lunch on me."

"Sorry," Missy muttered. "I've got a lot to carry." She stopped the plates from sliding and tried to step gently over the cafeteria bench. But her left toe got stuck. She tried to catch her balance, but it was too late.

"Watch out, Stephanie," Ashley shouted.

That was too late too.

Missy's arms flew up. Her tray flipped over, landing right on Stephanie's head. The plates crashed onto the table, onto the floor, and all over Stephanie.

"Hey!" screamed Stephanie. She looked down.

The creamed spinach covered her sweater. Gooey green dripped down from her bangs.

The other students in the cafeteria turned to see what had happened. A few older kids shouted, "Food fight! All *riiight*!" But one of the little kids yelled, "Oooooh! *Blood!*"

Stephanie touched her head and screeched when her hand came back sticky and red. She put her hand to her head again—this time it came back full of spaghetti. Red tomato sauce oozed down her neck and shoulders.

Stephanie turned to Missy. "My hair!" she cried. "My sweater! You've ruined everything!" Stephanie shot up from her seat, but her foot landed on a meatball. She slipped, tried to grab the table, but grabbed on to some creamed spinach instead. She flopped facedown on the table.

The whole cafeteria was staring at her—and at Missy—and laughing hysterically!

Stephanie pulled herself up, hid her face in her hands, and ran to the bathroom. The rest of the girls got up quickly and followed her.

Missy stared, horrified. "But . . ."

"You should try to be more careful, Missy," said Ashley, as she walked away.

Missy was left all by herself at the lunch table. She could feel everyone looking at her. Slowly, Missy turned over her lunch tray—and found her ice-cream bar, safe and sound. She picked it up. "Maybe some ice cream would cheer up Stephanie," she thought.

Missy walked into the bathroom and found Stephanie standing by one of the sinks. The rest of the girls were huddled around her. Stephanie's eyes were puffy from crying. Someone had tried to rinse the spaghetti sauce out of her hair, but that only made things worse.

"Go away, Missy," said one of the girls. Wilhelmina? Missy wasn't sure. "Stephanie doesn't want to talk to you."

The cluster of girls grew tighter.

"It was an accident," Missy said. "Honest!"

Mrs. Kaufman walked in. "What's going on, girls?" she asked.

"Missy Fremont spilled her lunch all over Stephanie's hair," said Christine, pointing an accusing finger at Missy. "Can Stephanie call her mother to come pick her up?"

Mrs. Kaufman inspected the damage. "Would you feel better if you went home and changed?" she asked.

Stephanie gave Missy a dirty look and then nodded tearfully.

"I'll take her to the office," Emily offered. She put her arm around Stephanie's shoulder and led her out the door.

"All right, girls, get back to the cafeteria now," said Mrs. Kaufman.

The girls whispered among themselves as they left the bathroom. "Stupid girls," muttered Missy under her breath. She stood quietly for a moment and then slowly unwrapped the ice-cream bar. She took a few bites, but even a bar of ice cream couldn't hold back her tears.

"How'd your day go?" asked Mrs. Fremont during dinner.

"Okay," said Missy. She had decided it was pointless to talk to her mother about school. The only one who really understood her was Baby.

Mrs. Fremont looked around the table and smiled. "I have good news," she said. "I got a call from the school district this afternoon. I'll be teaching tomorrow."

"That's terrific, Pat," said Mr. Fremont. "Where?"

Mrs. Fremont looked at Missy and smiled. "Hills Point!" she said.

Missy gulped.

"And guess whose class I'll be teaching?" she continued, still looking at Missy.

"Mine?" said Missy weakly.

Mrs. Fremont beamed.

"What happened to Mrs. Kaufman?" asked Missy.

"She's attending a one-day conference," said Mrs. Fremont. "Won't this be fun?"

Missy groaned. "Mom! How can you say that? Everyone in the class already hates me. Do you know how embarrassing it will be to have *my mother* as the teacher?"

"I thought you'd like the idea." Mrs. Fremont sounded disappointed.

Missy pushed her food around her plate with her fork. "How could she do this to me!" Missy thought. "Things are bad enough already!"

"Can you change your mind?" she asked.

"It's too late," said Mrs. Fremont. "I've already accepted the job. Besides, I thought you'd be thrilled."

Missy threw down her napkin angrily. "Nothing's going right," she wailed. "I wish we'd never moved here." She ran to her bedroom and fell onto her bed, crying. Baby followed, but not even *he* could cheer up Missy this time.

A moment later she heard a knock at the door.

"I'm busy," said Missy crossly.

Mrs. Fremont walked in anyway. She sat beside Missy on the bed. "I have an idea," she said, stroking Missy's hair.

Missy rolled over and wiped away a tear. "What is it?"

"Why don't I introduce myself to the class by my maiden name? I'll be Miss Stewart for the day. That way, no one will ever find out that I'm your mother."

"Would you really do that?" said Missy tearfully.

"Sure! It'll be our secret." Mrs. Fremont smiled.

Missy gave her mother a hug. "Thanks, Mom," she said. "I really appreciate this."

Mrs. Fremont stood up. "Now that that's settled, let's go finish our dinner."

CHAPTER

6

"**G**ood morning, class," said Mrs. Fremont. "My name is Miss Stewart. I'll be substituting for Mrs. Kaufman today."

Missy glanced nervously around the room. She hoped her mother wasn't going to make a fool of herself. Teaching kindergarten was very different from teaching older kids.

Mrs. Fremont held up the class's American history book. "Mrs. Kaufman asked me to start the morning with a little quiz on last night's reading assignment."

The class groaned.

"No talking," said Mrs. Fremont. "Please take out a clean sheet of paper and a pencil."

"Psst! Psst!" someone hissed. Missy looked across the room. Emily was sitting up in her seat, her hand cupped over her mouth. She was looking straight at Stephanie Cook.

"Young lady, what is your name?" said Mrs. Fremont.

"Emily," came the muffled reply.

"I thought I asked everyone to stop talking," said Mrs. Fremont.

Emily's face turned red.

"First question," said Mrs. Fremont. "What was the Stamp Act?"

There was some rustling by the door. Missy peeked over at Emily again. Then she glanced at Stephanie. She was relieved to see that Stephanie's hair was back to normal. All of a sudden, Missy noticed that Stephanie was making hand signals to Emily. Missy watched more closely. Sign language! Stephanie was using sign language to spell out the answers for Emily!

"Question two," said Mrs. Fremont. "Why did Paul Revere go on his famous midnight ride?"

Missy looked up at her mother. Would she notice the two girls cheating on the test? Mrs. Fremont moved closer to Stephanie's desk. "Question three," she said casually.

Missy lowered her eyes to her paper.

Mrs. Fremont reached down and took Stephanie's paper away. "I don't think I have to remind anyone that cheating is not allowed," she said. She turned Stephanie's desk around so that it faced the window and returned her paper.

Stephanie made a face and hunched over her desk with a loud huff.

"Shall we continue?" Mrs. Fremont asked. No one in the class said a word.

The last part of the quiz was an essay question about the Declaration of Independence.

Missy raised her hand.

"Yes?" said Mrs. Fremont.

"I don't understand the question," Missy said.

Mrs. Fremont walked over to her desk. "Just do the best you can," she said.

"But Mom!" Missy muttered. She stopped and froze. Missy hoped no one in the room heard her. She looked around the class. Everyone was busy writing. Everyone except Stephanie Cook.

Stephanie looked at Mrs. Fremont and then at Missy. Missy quickly lowered her eyes and started to write furiously. Had Stephanie heard? Missy wasn't certain. She could be sure of one thing, though. If Stephanie figured it out, Missy's secret was over.

"That substitute teacher sure is strict," said Emily during lunch.

"I like Mrs. Kaufman better," sniffed Wilhelmina, whose nickname, Missy had learned, was Willie.

Ashley groaned. "She'll probably assign us twice as much homework. I hope Mrs. Kaufman comes back soon."

Missy quietly ate her Sloppy Joe and pretended she was invisible.

But Stephanie was giving her a peculiar stare. "She looks familiar to me," she said suddenly. "Didn't she substitute at Hills Point last year?"

Missy cringed. Of *course* Mrs. Fremont looked familiar. Stephanie had probably seen her around their neighborhood!

Missy stood up quickly. "Excuse me," she said. "I left something in the classroom." She hurried down the hall and knocked on the door of the teachers' lounge.

Mrs. Pierce, the art teacher, answered the door. "Yes?" she said.

"Is Miss Stewart in there?" asked Missy. "It's important."

Mrs. Fremont came to the door.

"Mom," whispered Missy, "can you maybe wear a wig at home for the next few months?"

"What are you talking about?" asked Mrs. Fremont.

"Remember the blond girl who was cheating on the test?"

Mrs. Fremont nodded.

"Her name is Stephanie Cook, and she lives on our block," Missy explained. "I think she recognizes you!"

Mrs. Fremont frowned. "Oh, don't be silly, Missy! I'm tempted to speak to her parents anyway," she said. "That kid is rude and dishonest."

Missy grabbed her mother's arm. "Mom, please," she said. "If Stephanie recognizes you, she'll tell *everyone.*"

"Missy," said Mrs. Fremont firmly. "I am *not* going to walk around the neighborhood in a disguise. Don't you think you could speak to Stephanie in private and explain your situation?"

"Are you kidding?" said Missy. She looked down the hall. "Gotta go," she said. "Here they come."

"Missy," called Stephanie. "Wait. We want to talk to you."

Missy ignored them, hurrying ahead of them up the hall. She could hear everyone running to catch up. She looked around frantically, turned a corner, and slipped into the janitor's closet. Missy listened to the footsteps as the girls hurried by.

The footsteps stopped. "Please don't find me," she whispered to herself.

The closet door opened.

Missy grabbed a bucket and a sponge.

"Hi," she said casually. "I'm just about to wash the blackboard. Anyone want to help me?" As she walked out the door, Stephanie grabbed her elbow.

"Is Miss Stewart your mother?" Stephanie asked.

The girls waited expectantly.

Missy drew in a deep breath. "She's a friend of the family," she said quickly.

"Why have I seen her at your house so much?" said Stephanie suspiciously.

Missy lowered her voice. "If you promise not to tell, I'll let you in on a secret," she said. The girls huddled closer. "Miss Stewart recently lost everything she owned in a terrible fire. Her home, her car, her tiny dog, Buttons . . . If it weren't for my parents, she would have been stranded out on the street."

The girls heaved a collective sigh of pity. "That's terrible," said Willie. "No wonder she's so strict."

"Are you making this up?" Stephanie asked suspiciously.

Missy shook her head. "She didn't have any insurance or anything. She's going to stay with us until her finances are straightened out."

"I don't believe you," said Stephanie.

Emily turned on her. "That's a horrible thing to say," she said. "Why would Missy lie?"

"Poor Miss Stewart," Missy continued. "She even has to borrow my mom's clothes."

"Where does she sleep?" asked Wilhelmina.

"On a cot in the basement," Missy answered. "I

offered to share my room with her, but she prefers the privacy."

"That's stupid," said Stephanie. She looked at her friends. "Are you going to believe this?"

No one answered.

"My parents have friends whose house burned down," said Ashley. "It was awful."

"I'm going to the playground," Stephanie interrupted. "Is anyone coming with me?"

Silence. At last, Emily turned to Missy. "I'll help you wash the blackboard," she said.

"Me, too," chorused the other girls.

Stephanie gave Missy a dirty look. "Then I guess I'm going to the playground alone." She crossed her arms.

Just then, Mrs. Fremont walked past. "Hello, girls," she said, smiling.

"Oh, how *are* you, Miss Stewart?" asked Emily.

"I'm fine," said Mrs. Fremont. "Why?"

"We're about to clean the blackboard," Missy said loudly.

Mrs. Fremont looked at her watch. "Better hurry," she said. "Recess is almost over."

"Miss Stewart is *very* sensitive about her *situation*," Missy whispered as her mother walked away. "I wouldn't say anything to her about the fire."

"Poor Miss Stewart," said Ashley. "Maybe there's something we can do to help her."

By that afternoon, the whole class knew Miss Stewart's "secret." And everyone wanted to help. Christine suggested that they hold a clothing drive. "I know my mom has a lot of things that don't fit her anymore," she said.

Adam Ramirez offered to donate some old pots and pans, and Tommy Lawson pitched in his mother's bedroom lamp, which was stored in their basement. Of course, all donations would have to be brought to Missy's house, where "Miss Stewart" was staying.

"We really don't have the room for all this stuff right now," Missy protested.

But no one paid any attention to her.

When the three o'clock bell rang, Christine and Willie ran to Missy's mother and offered to carry her books to the car.

All the other girls except Stephanie joined them.

"Thank you, girls," said Mrs. Fremont.

"We hope you come back soon," said Kate.

"It'll help keep your mind off Buttons," Ashley added.

Emily nudged Ashley in the ribs.

"Buttons?" said Mrs. Fremont.

"Someone said you like to sew," Missy said quickly.

Mrs. Fremont looked puzzled.

Stephanie, who was combing her hair on the other side of the room, stopped. She looked at Missy, then at Mrs. Fremont.

"Time to go," said Missy quickly.

"Wait a minute," said Stephanie. She walked over to Mrs. Fremont. "Did you ever have a puppy named Buttons?" she demanded.

"No. Why?" replied Mrs. Fremont.

"What about the fire where you lost everything?" Stephanie continued.

"Shh!" said Christine.

"I don't know what you're talking about," said Mrs. Fremont.

"We thought you lost everything you had in a terrible fire," Ashley piped up. "Your home, your furniture, your tiny dog, Buttons . . ."

Missy's face was growing redder and redder.

Mrs. Fremont put her hands on her hips. "Melissa Fremont, are you behind this?" she asked.

Missy shrugged her shoulders.

"I knew it," cried Stephanie. "This *is* your mother, isn't it?"

The class was silent. Mrs. Fremont gave Missy a stern look.

"You lied to us!" Ashley said with a gasp.

"I knew it!" Stephanie repeated.

"But you don't *look* like Miss Stewart," Willie said to Missy.

"And you have different last names," Meredith added.

"I was adopted," Missy said glumly. "And Stewart is my mother's maiden name."

"What about all the clothes we were planning to collect?" said Christine.

"I guess you don't need my old bed now," added David Holt.

"Your *bed*?" said Mrs. Fremont.

Missy wanted to drop into a large hole and disappear.

"Missy told us you slept on a cot in the basement," said David.

"Missy!" said Mrs. Fremont.

"Come on, Emily," said Stephanie. "We're late for the bus." She grabbed Emily's arm and flounced out of the room.

The rest of the class quickly followed. Missy and her mother sat quietly for a few minutes.

"Melissa Fremont," her mother said, "I think you have some explaining to do."

CHAPTER

7

Missy's mother made her eat dinner alone in her room that night. Not even Baby was allowed to join her. Worse, she was grounded for the next week. No TV and no playing outside.

After dinner, there was a knock on the door. "Who is it?" asked Missy.

Mr. Fremont and Baby walked in. "I thought you could use some company," he said.

"Thanks," Missy replied gloomily. Mr. Fremont moved Missy's tray aside and sat down on the bed. "You didn't eat very much," he remarked.

"Baby can have it," said Missy.

"Tough day?" asked Mr. Fremont.

Missy rolled over and faced the wall.

"Say, did you hear the good news?" said Mr. Fremont after a bit. "Your mom has a job teaching kindergarten at the Iroquois Trails School until Christmas. She starts tomorrow."

Missy didn't answer.

Mr. Fremont stood up and shifted from one foot to the next. "Want me to take your tray?" he said finally.

Missy shook her head. "Sorry, Dad," she said, "but I just don't feel like talking right now."

"You know your mom and I love you," he said. "Whenever you're ready to talk, we're ready to listen."

As soon as Mr. Fremont left the room, Missy pulled her dinner tray closer. "Have some chicken, Baby," she said. "I know how much you like chicken."

Baby gulped down the food.

Missy stared at him and sighed. "I'm so embarrassed," she said. "Why can't I be *normal* like the other kids? It's bad enough being the new girl, but now I'll bet everyone thinks I'm really weird because I lied about my own *mother*. And besides *that*, now they know I was adopted!"

Baby put his paws on Missy's shoulders and licked her nose.

"It's true," she insisted. "After what happened today, I can't possibly show my face at Hills Point again."

Missy lay on her back and stared at the ceiling. "I wish I didn't have to go to school," she said. "I wish I could just stay home all day with you." Baby nuzzled his nose in Missy's face. Suddenly, Missy sat straight up. "Hey, wait a minute," she said. "Maybe I *don't* have to go to school after all. I just had a great idea!"

*   *   *

Missy hummed cheerfully as she got dressed the next morning.

"Hi, Mom. Hi, Dad. What's for breakfast?" she asked as she burst into the kitchen a few minutes later.

Mr. Fremont did a double take. "Is this the same daughter I spoke to last night?" he said.

Melissa grinned. "I'm feeling better," she said. "Congratulations on your new job, Mom," she added.

Missy ate quickly, then kissed her parents and Baby good-by.

"Have a nice day," said Mrs. Fremont.

"I will," Melissa replied cheerfully. She gave a little wave and hurried out the front door.

As soon as the door closed, Missy dropped to her knees and crept behind the thick row of bushes that hugged the front of the house. Soon she heard the school bus arrive across the street.

Using her book bag as a seat cushion, Missy settled down behind the bush with a library book. A few minutes later, Missy heard her mother drive away. "So far, so good," she whispered. She looked at her watch. "One more hour until Dad leaves for rehearsal."

Missy heard the front door open. She quickly shrank back. The next thing she felt was Baby's furry nose in her face. "Shoo," whispered Missy. "Go back inside."

"Baby," called Mr. Fremont. "Where are you?"

Missy shoved Baby away. "Go," she hissed. *"Now!"*

Mr. Fremont stepped off the front stoop. "Did you find something in the bushes, boy?" he asked.

Missy held her breath.

Baby barked one last time and ran up the front steps. "Good boy," said Mr. Fremont.

The front door slammed shut.

Missy started to breathe more easily.

The next hour seemed to last forever. Finally, Missy heard a car horn honking. Soon her father drove off in his car pool with some friends from the orchestra. Missy stood up and stretched.

"Baby, I'm home!" she called as she unlocked the front door. "No more school for Missy Fremont!"

Baby ran to her and barked noisily.

"And now for my brilliant idea," Missy announced dramatically. In her mother's room Missy found some peach-colored notepaper. Then in her mother's best handwriting she wrote:

Dear Mr. Lewis:

Melissa will be unable to attend school for several months. We have just learned that she is suffering from a very rare, contagious disease. Please have Mrs. Kaufman send all her schoolwork home until further notice.

Sincerely,
Patricia Fremont

P.S. I enjoyed teaching Melissa's class the other day.

Melissa looked up *contagious* in the dictionary to make sure she spelled it correctly. Then she carefully sealed the envelope and stuck it into the mailbox for the letter carrier to pick up.

Later Missy and Baby settled down in the armchair with cheese sandwiches, carrot sticks, and sodas. "Which soap opera would you like to watch first?" asked Missy. "How about *Loving Legends*?" She pressed the remote control and took a bite of her sandwich. For the first time in days, things were starting to go her way.

Melissa was in her room bent studiously over her math book when her mother returned home. "How were your kindergartners, Mom?" she asked.

"Great," Mrs. Fremont replied. "They're a really good class." She peered down the hall. "Is your father home from rehearsal yet?"

Missy shook her head. Her father usually rehearsed at the symphony hall every day from nine-thirty to three o'clock. He had performances on Friday and Saturday evenings and Sunday afternoons. Twice a year, the symphony went on a two-week tour, usually to exciting places like New York City and Boston.

"I thought we could look for wallpaper for your bedroom this weekend," said Mrs. Fremont. "Interested?"

"I thought I was grounded," Missy replied.

Mrs. Fremont smiled. "Consider this time off for good behavior."

The front doorbell rang. "Would you get that?" asked Mrs. Fremont. "I want to put in a load of wash."

Missy panicked. Suppose it was someone from school? The bell rang again.

Missy hurried to the front door. "Who is it?" she asked.

"Is Mrs. Fremont home?" said a tiny voice.

Missy opened the door. A little boy clutching a *Beginning Piano* book smiled, revealing a missing front tooth.

Missy relaxed. "Mom, it's one of your piano students," she called. She led the boy into the living room. "Mrs. Fremont will be here in a minute," she told him.

Missy went back to her room and shut the door. Baby had already crawled halfway under Missy's bed. "Take it easy, Baby," said Missy. "He hasn't even started to play yet." Baby whined. The *plink-plunk* of Mrs. Fremont's beginning piano students drove him crazy.

The doorbell rang a second time. "Not another one," Missy groaned. She threw the door open. "Stephanie!" she gasped. She slammed the door shut. What was *she* doing here? Checking up on Missy, probably. Bossy, stuck-up, *nosy* Stephanie!

Missy opened the door a tiny crack. "Be careful," she warned. "I have a contagious disease."

Stephanie stepped back. "Is that why you weren't in school today?" she asked.

"Yes. It's a really terrible disease," Missy said solemnly. "I must have brought it with me from Cincinnati."

"How long are you going to be out of school?"

"Months," Missy replied. "Maybe years."

Stephanie's eyes narrowed. "How do I know you aren't lying?" she asked. "You don't look sick."

"Oh, but I am! I have sacitis pleurum," Missy replied indignantly. One of the characters on *Loving Legends* had had that disease. Missy was glad she'd remembered the name of it. "So far the boils are only on my back," she added in a low voice.

"Boils?" said Stephanie. She moved back another few inches.

Missy opened the door a bit wider. "They'll be spreading to my hands soon," she said. She thrust her right hand at Stephanie. "Do you see any starting?"

"Gross," said Stephanie. "Don't touch me."

Missy pulled her hand back inside. "The worst part of this disease is when it reaches your hair. Once your scalp is covered with scales, your hair starts to fall out in big clumps."

Stephanie gasped. "I think I'll be going," she said quickly. "I hope you feel better soon."

"Thanks," replied Missy, "but I wouldn't count on it." She slammed the door triumphantly—right in Stephanie's face.

CHAPTER

8

The next day, Missy got
a phone call from Mr. Lewis, the school principal.

"Good morning, Missy," he said. "May I speak
with your mother?"

"She's in the shower," Missy replied.

"Oh," said Mr. Lewis. He cleared his throat.
"We received her note," he continued. "What exactly do you have?"

"Sacitis pleurum," Missy replied. "It's very rare."

"I'm sure it must be. How are you treating it?"

Missy wound the telephone cord around her
finger. "Antibiotics," she replied. "Lots of antibiotics."

Mr. Lewis paused. "I'd really like to speak to
your mother about this," he said. "Would you have
her call me as soon as possible? In the meantime,
I'll have Mrs. Kaufman arrange to send your schoolwork home."

Missy bit her lower lip. "Okay," she said. "Thanks,

Mr. Lewis." She quickly hung up the phone. It was Friday. Maybe Mr. Lewis would forget all about her over the weekend.

Saturday was hot and sunny. Missy and her mother were getting ready to go shopping for wallpaper. Missy stepped outside and pulled down the brim on her father's favorite baseball cap.

"Isn't that hat a little large for your head, dear?" asked Mrs. Fremont.

"I *like* this hat," Missy answered. She couldn't tell her mother that the hat was really a disguise.

Mrs. Fremont grimaced. "So does your father," she said. "Just don't lose it, okay?"

Missy nodded and looked back at the house. "May I bring Baby?" she said. "Please? He loves the car."

Mrs. Fremont frowned. "It's eighty-five degrees today. He'll be too hot."

"I'll bring some water along and leave the windows open," said Missy. "Please? He hasn't been out since I was grounded."

"Oh, all right," replied Mrs. Fremont with a smile. "Let's take him along."

Missy ran inside to get Baby. They both tumbled into the back seat of the car, and Mrs. Fremont drove off. Missy rolled down all the windows and stretched out. It felt great not to be cooped up in the house.

Wilson's Home Decorating Center was a huge place. It had everything from lumber to lighting fixtures. "I'll meet you in the wallpaper department," said Mrs. Fremont, taking a shopping cart. "But first I want to check the paint sale."

Missy carefully made her way down an aisle. There were hundreds of wallpaper patterns to choose from. She quickly narrowed her choice to three, but couldn't decide which one she liked the best. Then she looked around the store. Missy guessed that no one would mind if she brought Baby inside for a few minutes. She really needed his opinion.

Missy ran to the car. "Come on, Baby," she said. She snapped on his leash and quickly led him past the automatic doors.

The store manager immediately ran over to them. "Excuse me," he said. "No dogs allowed in the store except guide dogs."

"But I need his opinion," Missy replied. "It'll take only a minute."

The man folded his arms across his chest. "Sorry. No exceptions," he said.

"Okay," Missy sighed. She turned around—and stopped dead. There, less than three feet away and walking through the automatic doors, was Ashley Woods.

Missy pulled her cap over her eyes and spun back around. "Excuse me," she muttered, brushing past the manager.

"Hey!" he shouted. "I told you—no dogs. You can't come in here."

Baby raced down the garden supply aisle with Missy close behind. Suddenly, Baby's leash slipped out of Missy's grasp.

"Come back here," yelled the manager. He ran past Missy and grabbed Baby by the collar. With a noisy yelp, Baby squirmed loose and raced to the end of the aisle. As he rounded the corner, he knocked over a display of bamboo rakes.

"Wait for me," puffed Missy, running past the manager. She peered out from beneath her baseball cap and tried to see where she was going. There was a loud clatter as she stumbled over the rakes.

"Baby, where are you?" Missy whistled loudly, and as Baby came streaking back around the corner, she managed to grab his leash. "Let's get out of here," she said. They dashed through the bath accessories department.

"Watch out!" screamed a woman with a shopping cart.

Missy swerved around the cart, narrowly missing a pile of beach towels.

"Which way is the exit?" Missy asked breathlessly.

"Two aisles over and to your right," said the woman, pointing. "Next time, look where you're going."

"Sorry," Missy called over her shoulder. Baby whimpered and tried to wriggle free from Missy's tight grip.

"Quiet, Baby," whispered Missy. "People are staring."

Just as Missy neared the exit, Baby squirmed out of his collar. "Come back here!" Missy cried. But Baby sped off again.

Missy managed to catch up to him as he turned a wide corner. She lunged forward. "Gotcha!" she said.

But Baby lurched sideways, and he *and* Missy crashed right into Ashley Woods.

Ashley looked at Missy and turned white.

"It's okay," said Missy. "Relax."

Ashley screamed and covered her face. "Someone help me," Ashley yelled. "I've just been contaminated."

Missy turned and saw the manager and Mrs. Woods running toward them. Several people had stopped to watch. Missy replaced Baby's collar and leash as quickly as she could.

Ashley was clutching her head and shrieking something about her hair falling out. "Get away from me," she told Missy frantically. She began to sneeze.

Missy struggled to her feet. As she and Baby flew out the door, they could hear Ashley's wails growing louder.

A few minutes later, Mrs. Fremont found Missy and Baby sitting in the car. "What happened to you?" she asked. "I thought we were supposed to meet in the wallpaper department."

"I didn't see anything I liked," Missy replied casually.

"Someone on the other side of the store went berserk," said Mrs. Fremont. "I was hoping you had seen what happened."

"No, Mom," said Missy sweetly. "I've been out in the car with Baby." She settled back comfortably in her seat. "Too bad we missed all the excitement."

CHAPTER

9

On Monday, Missy collected her first homework assignment from the mailbox. "It's about time," she told Baby. "I'm getting sick of TV."

The phone rang. "What if it's someone calling from school?" Missy thought. She picked up the receiver and answered in her deepest voice.

"Mrs. Fremont?" said a woman.

"Speaking," Missy replied.

"*The Indianapolis News* is offering a special subscription rate for new customers. Would you be interested?"

Missy put her hand over the receiver. "Baby, would you like to get the paper?" she asked.

Baby wagged his tail.

"We'll take it," Missy said. She hung up the phone.

Missy finished her homework quickly. "Now what?" she asked Baby. "It's only eleven o'clock."

Baby scratched on the front door.

"Sorry," said Missy. "We aren't supposed to be outside." She flipped on the radio. "Indianapolis is having record high temperatures this week," said the announcer.

Missy lay down on the couch and fanned herself with a magazine. "You're telling me," she said. She got up and poured herself a glass of water.

Baby scratched on the front door again and whimpered. Missy stared idly out the window. "Wouldn't it be neat to play under the hose for a while?" she asked.

Baby barked and jumped up and down.

Missy peeked out the window again. The street was empty. Who would see them? She ran to her room and put on her bathing suit. "Come on, Baby," she said. "We'll just go out for a few minutes."

Missy checked up and down the block to make sure the coast was clear. "Perfect," she said. She uncoiled the hose and turned the water on. She sprayed it all over her. The water felt cool and refreshing.

"Ahhh, this is the life!" she exclaimed. She leaned her head back and soaked her hair. Missy pointed the hose at Baby. "Watch out. I'm going to squirt you," she said.

"Hey," screamed a voice. "Watch what you're doing."

Missy dropped the hose. "Stephanie!" she cried. She was too shocked to move.

Stephanie wiped the water off her face and stared at Missy. "I thought you were sick," she said.

"I thought *you* were in school," Melissa countered.

"I have a dentist's appointment," Stephanie replied. "What's your excuse?"

Missy started to back toward her house. "Be careful," she warned. "I'm still contagious."

Stephanie squinted suspiciously at Missy. "What happened to your boils?" she said. "I thought they covered your back."

"They're going away," Missy replied uneasily. "Now we're waiting for my hair to fall out."

Stephanie boldly walked closer. "I don't believe you," she said. "Prove it."

Missy held out her arm. "Don't come any closer or you'll be sorry," she warned.

Stephanie leaned forward. "Your arm looks fine, and your hair looks as bushy as ever," she observed. "I don't see a single bald spot."

Missy coughed dramatically. "I'm a very sick person," she said.

"Faker," said Stephanie. "There's nothing the matter with you. You're just a big faker."

"Am not," said Missy.

"Are too. Wait till I tell everyone at school." Stephanie stuck her nose in the air and stalked away.

Missy watched helplessly for a few minutes and then ran inside and slammed the door.

That evening, Missy sat nervously in the living room.

"Are you expecting to hear from someone?" asked Mrs. Fremont. "You've been guarding that phone all evening."

"If you get any closer, it's going to bite you," Mr. Fremont added.

"Very funny, Dad," said Missy.

"I'll bet it's a boy calling," said Mrs. Fremont.

"Mother!" said Missy. "It is not!"

When the phone finally rang, Missy jumped six inches. "I'll get it," she said, running to the kitchen. She grabbed the receiver. "Fremont residence," she said in her low voice.

"How's my favorite granddaughter?"

Missy breathed a huge sigh of relief. "Grandma!" she said. "Are you calling from Cincinnati?"

"Of course, darling. I've missed you all so much! When are you coming to visit?"

Missy looked out into the living room at her parents' smiling faces. "Soon, I hope," she answered.

"How's school?" asked her grandmother. "Have you made some new friends?"

Missy bit her lower lip. "Well, sort of," she replied.

"Don't worry," said her grandmother. "It's just a matter of time until everyone sees what a great girl you are!"

Missy felt her eyes well up with tears. Her grandmother always had a way of making her feel special.

"Is your mother around?" Missy's grandmother asked.

"Sure. Just a sec . . . Mom, it's Grandma," Missy called.

It seemed as if Missy's parents were on the phone forever. Missy curled up on the living-room rug with Baby. Soon she was asleep, happily dreaming of Cincinnati and of Grandma.

Missy was awakened by the sound of the phone ringing. She sat up and rubbed her eyes. "I'll get it," she said in a half-asleep voice. But she was too late.

Missy heard Mrs. Fremont answer the phone in the kitchen. "She *what*?" said her mother.

Missy's eyes opened wide.

"You're kidding me," Mrs. Fremont went on. She called to Missy's father. "William, come here a minute."

Missy propped herself up on her elbow and tried to listen. She heard her parents talking in hushed voices in the kitchen. Then her mother said, "Thank you for calling, Mr. Lewis," and hung up the receiver.

Missy quickly lay back down and pretended to be asleep. It didn't do any good. Two seconds later, her parents were in the living room. "Missy," said her father, "you'd better get up. You've got a lot of explaining to do."

Mr. Lewis hadn't forgotten after all.

Missy's mother was furious. "According to Mr. Lewis," she said, "you haven't been in school since last Wednesday."

Missy squirmed uncomfortably and stared at the floor.

"Do you have anything to say for yourself?" demanded her father.

Missy shook her head glumly. It was pointless to try to explain.

"Tomorrow you go back to school," said Mrs. Fremont. "Is that clear?"

"Yes," mumbled Missy.

"And, this time, you're grounded for a month," she added.

That night, Missy lay in bed wide awake. How could she face the kids in her class? She was probably the laughingstock of the whole school.

After her parents had gone to bed, Missy snuck out of her room. Baby was sleeping just outside her door. "Here, boy," she called softly. Baby woke up and wagged his tail. "Come in here," she whispered. "We have to talk."

Baby jumped on Missy's bed and waited for her to shut the door. "Baby," she began, settling down next to him, "I've decided that I can't ever show my face at Hills Point again. The only place for you and me is back in Cincinnati."

Baby whimpered.

"It'll be okay," she said. "Once Mom and Dad get used to the idea, I'm sure they'll agree it's for the best. We can live with Grandma, and I can be friends with Kelly and Susan and go to my old school again. No one there thinks I'm weird."

Baby looked at Missy and cocked his head quizzically.

"We'll go tomorrow morning after Mom and Dad leave for work," she continued. "I think I have enough money saved up to buy two bus tickets."

Baby hopped off the bed and ran to the door.

"Not *now*," Missy hissed. *"Tomorrow."*

Baby ran back and crawled under the covers. "Good boy," Missy said. She snuggled up against his warm fur. "I'd never go anywhere without you, Baby. You're still my best friend. In fact, you're my only friend." Baby licked Missy's face. Missy lay back on the pillow. "Go to sleep," she whispered. "We've got a busy day ahead!"

CHAPTER

10

Missy was up early the next morning. By the time her mother called her to breakfast, she had already packed her suitcase and hidden it underneath her bed.

"You're quiet this morning," said Mr. Fremont.

Missy poured herself a second bowl of cereal. "I guess so," she answered. She looked at the clock and quickly finished her breakfast. "Gotta go, Mom and Dad," she said. She gave both her parents a good-by hug and hurried out the front door. "I love you," she said, and waved.

Missy took a deep breath and ducked behind the hedge. Minutes later the school bus stopped and picked everyone up.

Missy waited until her parents left, and then she hurried back into the house. "Let's get ready, Baby," she said. Missy went to the kitchen and quickly filled a paper bag with Baby's things. Next, she made them each a sandwich and some hard-boiled eggs. Missy looked around the house. "Is there anything we've forgotten?" she asked.

Baby barked impatiently. He grabbed Missy's wrist and pulled her into the bedroom. Baby pawed open the closet door and rummaged around.

"Our photo albums!" Missy said softly. "How could I leave *them* behind? Thanks, Baby!" She knelt down and gave him a big hug. "I'm going to miss Mom and Dad," she said quietly.

Missy took the albums and stood up. "But it would be worse if I had to go back to Hills Point," she said stubbornly.

She put her things by the front door and then looked up the name of a taxicab company in the phone book. She gave the taxi dispatcher her address and told him where she wanted to go. Then she took all of the money she had saved and carefully tucked it into one of her knee socks.

Just before Missy left, she sat down and wrote her parents a short note:

Dear Mom and Dad,

Baby and I have gone to live with Grandma in Cincinnati. I hope you don't get angry, but I have no choice.

Love,
Missy

Outside, a horn honked. Missy peeked out the window. "Let's go, Baby," she said. She ran to the cab and threw her things onto the back seat.

The cab driver stared at Baby. "You planning to take him?" he asked gruffly.

"Yes," Missy replied.

The driver frowned. "Does he bite?" he asked.

"Never."

"Okay." The driver sighed. "Get in."

The driver watched Baby for a moment through his rearview mirror. "If he throws up on my back seat, you're both getting out," he said.

"Don't worry, he won't," Missy replied. She almost told the cab driver that she was taking Baby to the International Dog Show finals, but decided against it. Her stories had gotten her into enough trouble. She was finished with lying—forever!

The bus station was in a part of Indianapolis that Missy had never seen.

"Is this the downtown section?" she asked the driver.

"It sure is," he said. He pointed to a tall stone pillar. "That's the War Memorial," he said. The cab driver drove past the War Memorial and down several side streets. Missy noticed that the fare was getting expensive.

Finally, the driver pulled into a dingy building lit with fluorescent lights. "Here we are," he said. Missy reached into her knee sock and paid the fare. With one hand on Baby's leash and the other on her suitcase, she hesitantly made her way through the terminal.

"When does the next bus leave for Cincinnati?" she asked the ticket teller.

"Twelve-twenty," said the unfriendly looking woman.

Missy checked the time. It was eleven o'clock.

"I'd like two tickets please," she said.

The woman leaned out the window. "One way?" she asked.

"Right," Missy replied.

The woman looked at Baby. "You're not planning to bring *him* with you, are you?" she said.

Missy tightened her grip on Baby's leash. "Yes," she said firmly.

The woman shook her head. "No way," she said. "We can't allow a dog that size on the bus. Where would we put him?"

"I'm buying him a ticket," protested Missy.

The woman frowned. "No dogs."

"But he *has* to come with me," said Missy.

The woman motioned to the next person in line. "May I help you?" she said loudly.

Missy frowned. "I'm not moving until you sell my dog a ticket . . . please," she said.

The woman let out an exasperated sigh. "If you want to bring your dog, he'll have to be checked as baggage," she said. "There's an extra shipping charge for that."

"I'll take it," Missy replied.

The woman handed her the tickets. "One other thing," she said. "He has to be in a box."

Missy groaned. "Where will I find a box to fit a sheepdog?" she asked.

"That's not my problem," snapped the woman. "Next."

Missy went outside and sat on the curb. "Now what?" she thought. She shared part of her sandwich and a hard-boiled egg with Baby. The neighborhood didn't look very friendly. Missy stood up and wiped the crumbs off her face. "Maybe we can find a box in one of these stores," she said, looking around.

Missy and Baby passed a shoe store, a drugstore, and a coffee shop. "I wish we were on the bus," Missy whispered. She glanced at a clock. "One hour left. Do you see anything, Baby?"

Baby barked and tugged on his leash. "Where are you taking me?" asked Missy. She walked a few more steps. "A clothing store?"

"May I help you?" said the salesman.

"Do you have any large boxes you don't need?" asked Missy.

The salesman reached behind the counter and pulled out a box to fit an overcoat or jacket. "How's this?" He smiled.

Missy looked at the box and then at Baby. "Too small," she said. "It has to fit my dog."

"Are you giving him away?" said the man. "He looks like such a nice dog."

"We're going to Cincinnati," Missy replied. "He has to be in a box to travel on the bus."

The man nodded. "I see," he said. "Why don't you try the appliance store? They'd have large boxes." He gave Missy the directions. "Good luck," he called, giving her a wave.

Inside the appliance store a tall man with glasses was writing something on a clipboard. Missy asked about the boxes. "Check in the back," he told her without looking up.

Missy made her way to the rear of the store, where she saw several empty boxes piled up by the back door. "Here's one that I'll bet will fit you," Missy said. She eagerly untangled it from the rest. "Hop in, Baby," she said.

Baby walked to the far side of the door and sat down.

"No, Baby, over here," said Missy. She patted the box.

Baby barked to be let outside.

Missy grabbed Baby's collar and pulled him over to the box. "Please, Baby," she said. "You want to go to Cincinnati, don't you?" As she gave another tug, Baby stiffened his front paws and growled.

Missy looked at the clock on the wall. "Come on," she said, grabbing the empty box. "We're going to miss our bus if we don't hurry. We'll finish this discussion later!"

At the bus station, people were lining up to get on the bus to Cincinnati. Missy carefully set the box down on its side in a corner. "Okay, Baby," she said, clapping her hands. "This is your last chance. Get in."

Baby lay down on the floor. Missy frowned. "Okay. You asked for it," she said. She walked around behind Baby and pushed. Baby didn't budge. "Let's try from the front," Missy said. She bent down and tugged on his collar. Baby curled his upper lip and growled.

Missy glanced over at the bus. All the other

passengers were already on it. "Last call for Cincinnati," the bus driver yelled.

"Baby, please," begged Missy. "Our bus is leaving."

Baby picked up Missy's suitcase by its handle and carried it to the door of the bus station. He sat down next to it and waited.

"No, Baby," said Missy. "You don't understand. Our home is in Cincinnati."

Baby rested his chin on Missy's suitcase and whimpered. Out of the corner of his eye, he watched the bus pull away.

"Baby!" said Missy. "Why are you doing this to me? I thought we were best friends." She stalked over to the ticket window. "Excuse me," she said, "when is the next bus to Cincinnati?"

"That's it for today," replied the woman behind the counter.

"But I have to see my grandmother," Missy said.

"Sorry." The woman closed the window with a slam.

Missy sank down onto the bench. Tears filled her eyes. Baby trotted over and sat down beside her. "Go away," Missy said crossly. "It's all your fault."

Missy looked down at the floor. Suddenly she saw a pair of tennis shoes standing in front of her.

"Hey, stranger," said a familiar voice.

CHAPTER

11

"**D**ad!" said Missy, looking up. "What are you doing here?" She quickly wiped away her tears.

Baby hopped to his feet and wagged his tail.

"I was hoping I'd find you here," he said. "I got a call from Mr. Lewis saying you weren't in school. I went home and found your note." He peered at Missy's suitcase. "Looks like I got here just in time."

"We missed our bus," Missy said glumly. "The next one doesn't leave until tomorrow."

"Any chance you'll reconsider?" said Mr. Fremont. "I make great French toast."

Missy stared at the floor.

"Hey! I know a terrific ice-cream parlor near here where we can discuss the matter further." Mr. Fremont looked around the bus station. "Besides," he added, "you can't stay here all night."

Baby tried to lick Missy's face. She pushed him away angrily.

"Did something happen between you two?" asked Mr. Fremont.

"It's all *his* fault that I missed the bus," Missy replied angrily.

"Hmm," said Mr. Fremont softly. "Do you think he was trying to tell you something?"

Tears filled Missy's eyes once more. "Dad, I can't go back to that school again. I just can't. Baby doesn't have to go to Hills Point, but I do."

"Missy," said her father, "we've all done things we regret. That's no reason to run away."

"But how can I ever expect those kids to accept me now?" she asked.

"Just try being yourself," said Mr. Fremont. "You're a pretty special person, you know. Besides, school's been in session for only *one week*. Why don't you give your classmates a chance?"

Mr. Fremont put his arm around Missy's shoulders. "And what about your mom and me?" he continued. "Do you think we'd really want you and Baby to go live with Grandma?"

"I guess Baby was just trying to watch out for me," Missy said. She buried her face in her father's chest. "Oh, Dad, I'm sorry. I've been thinking only of myself. Let's go home."

Mr. Fremont hugged his daughter. "That's my girl," he said. "Now, I don't know about you, but I could still use that ice-cream cone."

"Are dogs allowed in this ice-cream parlor?"

"I don't see why not." Mr. Fremont smiled at Missy and at Baby. "Let's go."

That night Missy lay awake in her bed thinking. She was happy to be home again, and her parents were certainly glad to have her back. But what would happen when she returned to Hills Point? Missy closed her eyes and tried to fall asleep. She'd find out soon enough.

The next morning, Missy grabbed her book bag and peeked out the living-room window. The kids were already waiting at the bus stop. She took a deep breath. "Here goes," she said. Missy gave Baby one last hug and then hurried across the street.

"Well, look who's here." Stephanie sniffed haughtily. "The big faker."

Adam and Tommy, the two boys who were usually fooling around, stopped what they were doing and rushed up to Missy. "Hey, did you really make everyone think you were sick?" asked Adam.

Missy swallowed hard. "Yes," she replied.

"Wow," said Tommy. "It must have been fun to skip school."

"Actually, it got a little boring," Missy said.

"I'd never get bored if *I* didn't have to go to school," said Adam.

The bus rolled up and everyone piled on. "Hi, Missy!" Emily waved to her from one of the seats in the back. "Come sit next to me. I want to ask you something."

"That's my seat!" said Stephanie.

"I didn't notice your name written on it," Emily replied. "Sit over there, next to Ashley."

Ashley blew her nose and slid over. Stephanie sat down with a noisy thud.

Emily turned to Missy and smiled. "What did

you do all the time you were home?" she whispered. "Was it fun?"

Missy couldn't believe it. The kids were actually interested in her escapade. "It was okay," she answered.

"I'm glad you're back," Emily continued. "Mrs. Kaufman assigned us a special history project, and I wanted to ask you to work on it with me."

"You did?" said Missy. "What about Stephanie? I thought she was your study buddy."

"You can't *always* do things with the same person," Emily replied. "Sometimes, it's a good idea to give a *new* person a chance!"

Missy sat back and smiled. Maybe her new school wouldn't be so bad after all. In fact, with a new friend like Emily and a best friend like Baby, maybe, just maybe, everything would be great!